Fans Love Reading
Choose Your Own Adventure®!

Watch for these titles coming up in the

CHOOSE YOUR OWN ADVENTURE®

Dragonlarks™ series

Ask your bookseller for books you have missed
or visit us at cyoa.com to learn more.

YOUR VERY OWN ROBOT
by R. A. Montgomery
INDIAN TRAIL
by R. A. Montgomery
CARAVAN
by R. A. Montgomery
THE HAUNTED HOUSE
by R. A. Montgomery
YOUR PURRR-FECT BIRTHDAY
by R. A. Montgomery
GHOST ISLAND
by Shannon Gilligan
SAND CASTLE
by R. A. Montgomery

MORE TITLES COMING SOON!

www.cyoa.com

SAND CASTLE

BY R.A. MONTGOMERY

A DRAGONLARK BOOK

Sand Castle © 1986 R.A. Montgomery
Warren, Vermont. All Rights Reserved.

Artwork, design, and revised text © 2008 Chooseco, LLC,
Waitsfield, Vermont. All Rights Reserved.

Illustrated by: Keith Newton
Book design: Stacey Boyd, Big Eyedea Visual Design
For information regarding permission, write to:

CHOOSECO
P.O. Box 46
Waitsfield, Vermont 05673
www.cyoa.com

A DRAGONLARK BOOK
ISBN: 1-933390-59-X
EAN: 978-1-933390-59-8

Published simultaneously in the United States and Canada

Printed in China.

0 9 8 7 6 5 4 3 2 1

For Ramsey, dearly loved.

A DRAGONLARK BOOK

READ THIS FIRST!!!

WATCH OUT!
THIS BOOK IS DIFFERENT
than every book you've ever read.

Don't believe me?

Have you ever read a book that was about YOU?

This book is!

YOU get to choose what happens next
—and even how the story will end.

DON'T READ THIS BOOK FROM
THE FIRST PAGE TO THE LAST.

Read until you reach a choice.
Turn to the page of the choice you like best.
If you don't like the end you reach, just start over!

"One more turret, that's what it needs," you say out loud as you stand back and look at your huge sand castle. Just then your father calls you. "Time for dinner. Hurry up."

"I'll be right there, Dad. Ten more minutes?" you reply.

"No! When I say now, I mean now. No stalling for time!"

"Oh, Dad, come on. I won't be long." You bend down and pick up your pail and shovel.

"Right now." Dad leaves the porch of your beach cottage and disappears inside.

You turn back to the castle. "Well, I guess you'll have to wait until morning, old sand castle. Dad won't let me back on the beach until tomorrow."

Turn to page 2.

During dinner your father and mother talk about the storm-warning flag that's been raised at the Coast Guard station. "I haven't seen that flag fly all summer," your mom says.

"It's going to be a big blow, a really big blow," adds your father. The weather report says it will start after midnight. We'd better pull up the rowboat."

"What about my sand castle?" you ask.

"I'm afraid it will be washed away," your mom answers.

"Oh, no! It can't!" you say. "I won't let it!"

"You can't stop old Mother Nature," your father replies, giving you a friendly pat on the shoulder.

Turn to page 5.

"Sorry. This is hard work," you say.

The boy begins to cry. Sitting in the sand with tears on his cheeks, he looks so unhappy that you change your mind.

"I was only kidding. Of course you can help. I need all the help I can get."

For the rest of the day you and your new friend work and work until the sand castle is even bigger than before.

"This is the best sand castle in the whole wide world," the boy says.

You proudly agree.

The End

Late that night you wake with a start and go to the window. Heavy, dark clouds are covering part of the moon. The wind is rising, and the ocean looks rough and foamy.

Suddenly, you hear a faint cry outside. "Help! Help!"

You press your ear to the window. You hear the sound again—and it sounds like it's coming from the castle!

If you decide to go down to the sand castle in the morning, turn to page 6.

If you decide to go out immediately, turn to page 9.

It's hard to sleep, so you sit up for a while. You can hear the wind howling outside and the rain beating against your window. Finally your eyes close, but you don't get much sleep. All night long you toss and turn and have lots of weird dreams.

When you wake up the next morning, the sun is streaming through the window. A few clouds dot the sky, but the storm is over.

You go to the window and look out. Half of your castle is gone. The back wall and two turrets and part of the main chamber have been washed away, but the flag is still flying above the tallest turret.

You rush down the stairs, out the door, and onto the beach. A small child you've never seen before is sitting in the sand next to your castle.

"Can I help?" he asks. "I've been watching you build the castle. It's really good."

If you decide to let him help you rebuild the castle, turn to page 13.

If you say, "No, you're too small," turn to page 4.

You pad lightly down the stairs. There's no sense in waking your parents, you tell yourself. They'd never believe that you heard a cry for help coming from the sand castle!

You tiptoe out the door and across the porch, and then run as fast as you can over the lawn onto the beach. Just as you reach the castle a huge wave rushes toward you. From inside the castle you hear a sharp cry. "Help, oh help! Please, someone help!"

Turn to the next page.

The wave crashes over you, knocking you off your feet. A tingling feeling like electricity spreads all through your body. The water must be some kind of magic potion! You feel yourself shrinking, and in minutes you're the size of a snail!

The castle walls tower above you. Only now it's a real castle—not one made of sand! Again you hear the cry for help, and this time it sounds even more pleading. You think you see a light in the main chamber of the castle up on the second floor. What should you do?

If you decide to return to your bedroom, turn to page 22.

If you decide to get some kind of help, turn to page 27.

If you decide to enter the castle, turn to page 30.

"Well...I guess we can always build a sand castle," you say. "It would be fun to explore the beach."

Marcelle pipes up. "I'll lead the way. I know some really exciting places."

"Like where?" you ask, a little miffed that she's trying to be the leader.

"Like the sunken ship, if you must know, or the haunted cove, which I'm sure you've heard of. You can decide where we go."

You think for a minute. You haven't been to either place, but both sound like fun!

If you decide to go to the sunken ship, turn to page 18.

If you decide to go to the haunted cove, turn to page 20.

"Sure," you reply. "Do you have any tools?"

The boy looks down at his feet in the sand, then answers, "Nope."

"Well, you'll need a shovel and pail. Why don't you get them from home?"

He scrambles to his feet and takes off down the beach.

Turn to the next page.

The boy runs past a sign that says NO TRESPASSING. Then he disappears around a bend where some black boulders are piled. You've never gone beyond the huge rocks. Your parents have often warned you not to wander on that private part of the beach.

About fifteen minutes later the boy reappears, and this time he has an older girl and boy with him. A big shaggy dog trails behind them. "This is my sister, Marcelle, and my brother, Biff," the boy says. "My name is Todd."

You shake hands and ask what the dog is named.

"We call him Lobster," Todd answers.

"Where do we start?" Biff asks.

But before you can reply, Marcelle says, "Hey, let's go exploring."

If you decide to rebuild the castle, turn to page 16.

If you decide to go exploring, turn to page 12.

You point to the spot where the rear wall and main chamber used to be. "There," you say. "This time let's line it with shells. Maybe that will stop the waves from wrecking it."

Hours later the four of you and Lobster sit down, tired but proud of the work you've done. The sand castle is bigger than before, with a moat all around it and four tall turrets.

"Why don't we build a tree house?" cries Todd.

"Yeah, great idea!" chimes in Marcelle.

"Let's meet here tomorrow. I'll bring tools," you say.

It looks as if this will be a great summer now that you have three new friends—and Lobster—to play with!

The End

Sunken ships have always interested you. No one says much as you trudge overland through pine and birch forest to get to the bluff. Marcelle claims that you can see the sunken ship from there.

An hour later you come out on the high bluff. It overlooks a rocky beach, where a freighter lies offshore. It's on its side, and there's a huge hole beneath the waterline. The metal plates are rusty and battered. Sea gulls perch on the wheelhouse railing, and waves slap the boat's hull with a hollow booming sound.

"See! I told you there was a sunken ship here," says Marcelle.

You don't answer her. You're too busy watching the boat's wheelhouse, where you think you see a figure moving about. There's something mysterious about this freighter, you tell yourself, and you know you'll be back to do some real exploring…

The End

"I'm not afraid of haunted coves or haunted houses or anything," you say loudly. "Lead the way."

"You'll see," is all Marcelle says as she starts off at a fast pace. You follow her onto the private beach. Fifteen minutes later you come to a small cove. You see a white boathouse with peeling paint and lots of missing windows. No one is in sight.

"Spooky, isn't it?" Marcelle says. "I dare you to go in."

If you decide to accept her dare, turn to page 50.

If you dare her to lead the way, turn to page 40.

You turn around and trudge over the giant sand dunes toward your house. Finally you reach a lush green forest—your lawn! Your journey across it is slow, difficult, and dangerous. Twice you are forced to hide when a patrol of army ants marches past. And other insects live in the lawn: huge, dinosaurlike bugs that look at you hungrily as you pass.

Turn to the next page.

With great courage you push on until dawn. The storm has ended, and the sun beats down on the rain-soaked grass. You barely make it to the porch of your house.

"What now?" you cry, looking up. "I'll never make it up these steps."

You rest for a minute in the sun. But when you wake up, you are normal-size and in your bed!

"Just a dream," you say, feeling your arms and legs, just to be sure. Then you rush to the window and look out to where the sand castle was. It's gone!

"Well, I'll have to start over," you say, and settle back into the comfort of your bed.

The End

"There must be someone who can help," you say to yourself in a half whisper.

"What's that? You need help? Why? When? Where? And who are you anyway?" says a squeaky voice behind you.

You jump and turn around. It's a fiddler crab. And because of your new small size, it towers over you!

Turn to the next page.

"I'm me. I live in that house up there," you say, pointing.

"A likely story," the fiddler crab answers. "You're too small to be a human! What's this about help?"

"I think someone needs help in the castle. Will you come with me?" you ask.

The crab thinks for a moment. "Okay, but I'm a coward. If we do anything dangerous, I'll run away. Be warned."

Just then, a porch light goes on at the cottage, and your father yells, "Hey, where are you? Come in. This storm is fierce."

If you decide to go back in the house, turn to page 32.

If you decide to enter the castle, turn to page 34.

Another wave crashes against the back wall of the castle, and you hear the gurgle of the seawater as it rushes back down the beach to the sea.

You walk quickly through the castle's entrance gate, cross the soggy sand courtyard, and enter the main chamber.

Inside the sand castle is a beautiful room with rugs on

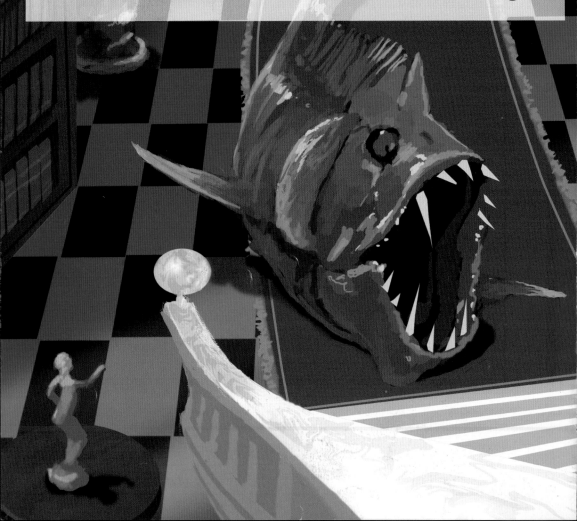

the floor, pictures on the walls, and heavy, dark furniture. You can't believe it.

"Help!" It's the cry again, and it's coming from upstairs. You cross the room and start up a marble staircase. You hear a strange noise and whirl around sharply. An electric eel is sliding toward you, clacking its sharp teeth.

If you try to battle the eel, turn to page 39.

If you run upstairs, turn to page 48.

"COMING!," you yell in your loudest voice, but that isn't very loud anymore.

Suddenly a wave knocks you down, and you fight against the rushing water. You gasp for air and twist and turn in the swirling green sea.

"Hey, what's going on?" you yell. Again the tingling feeling shoots through your arms and legs. You're back to your normal size! The magic potion must have worn off.

As you climb to your feet waves smash over the sand castle. Little by little, bits of the sand castle topple until all that's left is a hump in the sand where the main hall once stood. You turn away sadly and go home, where you get a lecture from your mom and dad—and a cup of hot cocoa.

The End

"Come on, Crab," you say. "There's no time to lose. Someone needs our help!"

You turn to the house and yell, "Be back in a minute, Dad. Don't worry." But you have forgotten how tiny you are now. Your voice is lost in the noise of the storm.

"I don't like this. I don't like it one tiny bit," the crab says as you lead the way into the courtyard of the castle.

Turn to the next page.

Suddenly three men in armor dash out of the main guard room.

"Halt!" one of them yells, and bars your way with a lance. "What do you want?"

"Someone called for help," you reply, frightened by the stern looks on the faces of the men.

"No one needs help here. Be gone," the man says. He lowers the sharp, gleaming lance at you. His eyes flash with anger. You move two steps back. The guard moves even closer. You feel the tip of his lance on your chest.

If you retreat, turn to page 45.

If you argue with the armed men, turn to page 49.

You search for a weapon. On the wall before you is a broad old sword. You grab it and yell, "I'm ready for you, Eel.

"Take that, and that," you shout as you thrust with the sword. The eels slithers snake-like down the stairs and out of the castle into the pounding storm.

For now you are safe.

The End

"After you," you say politely.

"Don't be such a 'fraidy cat. Nothing will hurt you," Marcelle says. You both go through the door at the same time. Inside the boathouse you find six large leather trunks. They are filled with lots of old clothes—hats, jackets, pants, dresses. You find letters and yellowed family pictures.

"Maybe we should leave. This belongs to someone," you say.

"To us," Marcelle answers. "It's Granddad's stuff. We play here all the time. I was only kidding

about the place being haunted. Come on, try this on."

Turn to the next page.

And that's the beginning of the summer playhouse. You and your friends put on two shows in the old boathouse. Only your parents come to the first one, but word spreads fast. Twenty-two people watch the second show, a play you star in. You are a great success.

The End

You're confused—you just built this castle! But it must be magic, and magic is a funny thing. You glance at the wall, and sure enough, there's a bunch of keys. You unlock the prisoners, and moments later the three of you flee the castle. You rush through the waves that are swirling around the courtyard. Finally you reach the safety of high ground. You huddle under a lawn chair as rain and wind sweep down.

"We'll straighten this out in the morning. Thank heavens we're safe—at least for now," you say.

"The potion is wearing off," the girl exclaims suddenly. And before your very eyes, the three of you return to normal human size.

The End

"No problem," you say backing away. We're on our way. Just visiting."

Once you're safely outside the castle walls, you and the fiddler crab decide to tunnel into the castle under the side wall. It's connected directly to the main chamber. "Dig fast. We don't have much time, Crab," you say.

"You mind your own work. I'll do mine, don't you worry," he replies.

Just as you break through into the castle, you hear a bloodcurdling scream. The fiddler crab takes off without even saying goodbye!

Ahead you see a stairway that leans to an open door. Slowly you climb the stairs toward it. The door is open just a crack.

Turn to page 46.

You pull the door fully open, and enter the room. It's filled with chests of gold and jewels! And in the center of the room are two tiny children, a boy and girl. They are chained to a throne encrusted with rubies.

"Thank you for coming," the girl cries out. "We've been prisoners in this ratty old castle for three hundred and sixteen years. We were tricked by an old man who gave us a potion. We've been this size ever since! The key to these chains is on the wall over there."

Turn to page 44.

"I'm faster than you, Eel," you yell as you dash up the stairs.

At the top of the staircase there's a long, twisting corridor with dozens of closed doors. You're not sure where the cry for help is coming from.

You open door after door, but each room is dark and silent. Finally you spot a massive oak door with a golden handle. You tug on the handle, and the door creaks open. A pale, clear light is shining within.

Turn to page 46.

You glance sideways. The fiddler crab won't be any help—he's too busy digging a hole in the wet sand. A second later he ducks into the hole and you face the men alone. "Let me through!" you cry.

"Lock up the intruder," the leader shouts. Before you can act, you are dragged off to the dungeon in the smallest turret.

The men slam the door, and there you are—a prisoner in your own sand castle!

The End

"Nothing to it," you say bravely, marching up the old wooden steps to the boathouse. You push open the door, brushing cobwebs away, and step inside.

"YIKES!" you yell, and jump back.

"What is it?" asks Todd shakily. Biff runs and hides behind Lobster.

"Oh, nothing, I thought I saw someone in there," you reply.

"'Fraidy cat," Marcelle says. "Come on. It's just your imagination. It's our boathouse, anyway."

Go on to the next page.

Marcelle leads the way. There is no one in the boat-house, but it's dark inside. The wind howls through the cracked windows.

You're the first to speak. "I've had enough exploring. Let's go back and work on the old sand castle." The others look glad.

"Great idea," Todd cries, and you all run down the beach back to the castle.

The End

CREDITS

Illustrator Keith Newton began his art career in the theater as a set painter. Having talent and a strong desire to paint portraits, he moved to New York and studied fine art at the Art Students League. Keith has won numerous awards in art such as The Grumbacher Gold Medallion and Salmagundi Award for Pastel. He soon began illustrating and was hired by Walt Disney Feature Animation where he worked on such films as *Pocahontas* and *Mulan* as a background artist. Keith also designed color models for sculptures at Disney's Animal Kingdom and

has animated commercials for Euro Disney. Today, Keith Newton freelances from his home and teaches entertainment illustration at the College for Creative Studies in Detroit. He is married and has two daughters.

This book was brought to life by a great group of people:

Shannon Gilligan, Publisher
Gordon Troy, General Counsel
Melissa Bounty, Senior Editor
Stacey Boyd, Designer

Thanks to everyone involved!

ABOUT THE AUTHOR

At the Temple of Literature and National University
(Van Mieu-Quoc Tu Giam) in Hanoi, Vietnam

R. A. MONTGOMERY has hiked in the Himalayas, climbed mountains in Europe, gone scuba diving in Central America, and worked in Africa. He lives in France in the winter, travels frequently to Asia, and calls Vermont home. Montgomery graduated from Williams College and attended graduate school at Yale University and NYU. His interests include macroeconomics, geopolitics, mythology, history, mystery novels, and music. He has two grown sons, a daughter-in-law, and two granddaughters. His wife, Shannon Gilligan, is an author and noted interactive game designer. Montgomery feels that the generation of people under 15 is the most important asset in our world.

**For games, activities, and other fun stuff,
or to write to R. A. Montgomery,
visit us online at CYOA.com**

Original Fans Love Reading
Choose Your Own Adventure®!

The books let readers remix their own stories—and face the consequences. Kids race to discover lost civilizations, navigate black holes, and go in search of the Yeti, revamped for the 21st century!
***Wired* Magazine**

I love CYOA—I missed CYOA! I've been keeping my fingers as bookmarks on pages 45, 16, 32, and 9 all these years, just to keep my options open.
Madeline, 20

Reading a CYOA book was more like playing a video game on my treasured Nintendo® system. I'm pretty sure the multiple plot twists of *The Lost Jewels of Nabooti* are forever stored in some part of my brain.
The Fort Worth Star-Telegram

How I miss you, CYOA! I only have a small shelf left after my mom threw a bunch of you away in a yard sale—she never did understand.
Travis Rex, 26

I LOVE CYOA BOOKS! I have read them since I was a small child. I am so glad to hear they are going back into print! You have just made me the happiest person in the world!
Carey Walker, 27